Hello, Family Members,

Learning to read is one of the most important accomplishments of early childhood. **Hello Reader!** books are designed to help children become skilled readers who like to read. Beginning readers learn to read by remembering frequently used words like "the," "is," and "and"; by using phonics skills to decode new words; and by interpreting picture and text clues. These books provide both the stories children enjoy and the structure they need to read fluently and independently. Here are suggestions for helping your child *before*, *during*, and *after* reading:

Before

- Look at the cover and pictures and have your child predict what the story is about.
- Read the story to your child.
- Encourage your child to chime in with familiar words and phrases.
- Echo read with your child by reading a line first and having your child read it after you do.

During

- Have your child think about a word he or she does not recognize right away. Provide hints such as "Let's see if we know the sounds" and "Have we read other words like this one?"
- Encourage your child to use phonics skills to sound out new words.
- Provide the word for your child when more assistance is needed so that he or she does not struggle and the experience of reading with you is a positive one.
- Encourage your child to have fun by reading with a lot of expression . . . like an actor!

After

- Have your child keep lists of interesting and favorite words.
- Encourage your child to read the books over and over again. Have him or her read to brothers, sisters, grandparents, and even teddy bears. Repeated readings develop confidence in young readers.
- Talk about the stories. Ask and answer questions. Share ideas about the funniest and most interesting characters and events in the stories.

I do hope that you and your child enjoy this book.

— Francie Alexander
Reading Specialist,
Scholastic's Learning Ve

For all the children in Ms. Delia's Class 2-325
and Ms. Vega's Class 3-321B
at P.S. 291 in the Bronx (1998-1999)
—T. S.

To Leigh
—M. S.

ISBN 0-439-09910-2

Text copyright © 1999 by Teddy Slater.
Illustrations copyright © 1999 by Maggie Swanson.
All rights reserved. Published by Scholastic Inc.
SCHOLASTIC, HELLO READER, CARTWHEEL BOOKS and associated logos
are registered trademarks of Scholastic Inc.

Library of Congress Cataloging-in-Publication Data is available

10 9 8 7 6 5 4 3   0/0 01 02 03 04
                Printed in Mexico.   24
              First printing, September 1999

Busy Bunnies' Five Senses

by Teddy Slater

Illustrated by Maggie Swanson

Hello Reader! Science — Level 1

SCHOLASTIC INC. Cartwheel B·O·O·K·S ®

New York Toronto London Auckland Sydney Mexico City New Delhi Hong Kong

I taste with my tongue.

She smells with her nose.

We touch with our skin,
from fingers to toes.

He has two ears to hear with

and two eyes to see.

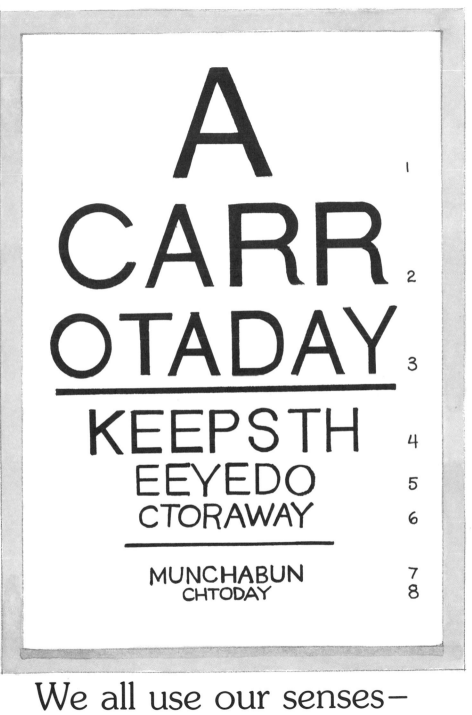

We all use our senses—
she, he, and we.

THE SENSE OF TASTE

Food can taste salty,

bitter,

or sour.

But the yummiest treat
is one that tastes sweet!

THE SENSE OF SMELL

You can tell by the smell
when a rose is in bloom.

Your nose knows when
something smells bad
in your room.

And here is a fact
we all know is true.
Your nose knows...

a skunk when it smells one.

THE SENSE OF TOUCH

Touch something smooth.

Touch something rough.

Touch hard things.

Touch soft things.

Oops!
That's enough.

THE SENSE OF HEARING

Clap your hands.
Stamp your feet.

Listen to the marching beat

Hear a whisper.

Hear a shout.

Hear what sound is all about.

Booming, banging,
jangly noise...
made by girls and boys.

THE SENSE OF SIGHT

Open your eyes
and what do you see?

A bright orange carrot,

a leafy green tree.

A small grain of sand,

and big starry skies.

The world's full of wonder.

Open your eyes!